SEAN

SHIFTER WORLD

ROYALS AND ALPHAS
BOOK FOUR

DANA ARCHER

FOREWORD BY
NANCY CORRIGAN

Hi there!

Nancy Corrigan here. I'm the real person behind Dana Archer. I'm also the owner, creator, and author of the stories in the Shifter World.

You've picked up the **closed-door romance version*** of Sean and Jenna's book, *Sean*. On these pages you'll enjoy a paranormal shifter romance with all the emotions, plenty of kisses, lots of growling, a bit of snarling, some "good guy" vs. "bad guy" fighting, and the **fresh and unique storyline** you expect from me.

My promise to you: no AI bots or ghostwriters were used in the writing of this story.

In this novel, I guarantee:
- No cheating!
- No cliffhanger!
- And a satisfying happy ever after.

Happy reading!

Nancy Corrigan

*If you'd rather read the original version of this story, grab *Chance on Love* by Nancy Corrigan.

CHAPTER ONE

Sean made another loop around the Kagan Industries' office and cursed. Pacing wasn't helping. Nothing he'd tried since sundown had. He hurt, plain and simple. His skin itched, and his bones ached. The sensation of claws raking the inside of his chest made it worse, but it wasn't the pain gripping him that left him angry. It was the obstinate wolf he housed.

The separate entity he'd been born with had its own wants and goals. At the moment, they conflicted with Sean's plans for the evening. Since he was ultimately in charge, the animal would just have to suck it up.

His wolf's snarl echoed within him. No doubt it disagreed. Not his problem. His wolf wasn't the only stubborn one, and Sean refused to allow his primal side to rule him. He would not make the same mistake his friend Nic had made .

Sean was too young to fall in love. Or in lust. Both could seal a shifter's fate.

Hands fisted, he strode for the window. As much as he wanted to ignore the full moon, he needed the strength it offered. He shoved the lace curtain aside and stepped into the swatch of moonlight.

Warmth infused him, and his wolf calmed. Momentarily, at least. Still, he'd take the brief reprieve. He had a long night ahead of him.

He leaned against the window frame and surveyed the little slice of West Virginia that had served as the Kagan pack's home since the early seventeen hundreds. Stone paths wove through gardens and around the large, man-made pond. Beyond the still water, a fountain and a gazebo offered a place to sit and relax. Farther out, trees marked the separation of the humans' town and their territory. Their communal land was beautiful. He loved every inch of it, but at the moment, he wanted to run as far and as fast as he could away from it.

"Greeting the full moon all alone again, huh?"

Noah's voice cut through the silence of the night.

Sean peered over his shoulder at his cousin. Protective instincts flared. "What are you doing here? Tanner males aren't allowed on Kagan pack lands."

"Worried about me?"

"Yes." As a member of their rival pack, Noah's presence could be constituted as a threat depending on who saw him. Sean knew better. Noah would give his life if it meant saving one of them. Sean would do the same for a member of Noah's pack.

Noah shut the door behind him. With his dark blond hair in a short ponytail and a white T-shirt stretched over his muscled chest, he garnered the attention of males and females alike. One glance into his deadened green eyes, however, and most people steered clear of him.

Guilt, anger, and loneliness gave him a don't-mess-with-me vibe that was hard to miss. Losing a female days after mating her would do that to any male. It gave Sean yet another reason to avoid their women.

"Technically, I'm not on your pack's lands. The Kagan office sits a few hundred feet inside the humans' town. As for why I'm here?" Noah leaned against the opposite side of the window. "Your alpha asked me to talk some sense into you."

About Sean's refusal to shift. Everyone in his pack had been on him about it. Their lectures had gotten old. "You're wasting your time. I'm fine. My wolf's fine. End of discussion."

"Is it?" Noah raised a brow. "You're not getting edgy? Irritable? Or feel like you're going to come out of your skin?"

If Noah considered insomnia and the new holes Sean had punched into his bedroom walls as fitting those criteria, then the answer would be yes. He shrugged. "Nothing I can't handle."

Noah made a noncommittal sound, then glanced out the window, scanning the property the way Sean had. "Any word on Nic? Is he coming home soon?"

"What? No warnings or long speeches about how I'll go insane if I don't let my wolf out?"

"Nope. You're not stupid. You're just an idiot."

Sean laughed. "Yeah? What's the difference?"

"You know the facts. You're just choosing to ignore them."

Noah had a point. Sean wouldn't deny that. He grunted and turned his attention to the backyard. "I'm not shifting until I'm sure I have control over my instincts."

"And when's that going to be?"

"Soon." Or not.

Silence descended in the room while his wolf's growls reverberated within him, building the pressure behind his eyes. Finally, Noah sighed, breaking the tense moment. "Well?"

"Well, what?"

"Nic? Any word from him?"

"He called this morning." Actually, Nic called every day with the same question—how's Riley? The human female Nic had fallen in love with and tried to mate had ruined him, but it wasn't her fault or his that she'd been born the wrong species. Fate had screwed them both and guaranteed, neither would be happy.

"Did he say when he's coming home?"

"Not until it's time for his dad to pass on our pack spirit. He wants to enjoy life before he has to pick a shifter female to mate. He's in no rush to be saddled with a breeding partner."

"Saddled? Well, that's a horrible way to look at it. Being mated is a wonderful experience."

"How would you know? Yours—" Sean groaned and dropped his head against the cool glass. "I'm sorry. That was uncalled for."

"And completely out of character for you." No anger darkened Noah's voice, only understanding. He laid a comforting hand on Sean's shoulder. "It's going to get worse. You need to shift and accept what you are. Fighting it is only going to make all your moods stronger, from ones of aggression to passion."

"You think I don't know that? It's why I've been fighting to get my wolf to obey me. Without Nic here..." He shook his head, disgusted by his instincts.

"Without Nic here to claim the spirit wolf from his aging father, you're driven to secure your position in the pack, so you can take over as alpha."

Noah voiced the truth that had plagued Sean since Nic took off. In Sean's wolf's eyes, Nic's absence offered Sean the opportunity to seize the most revered role a shifter could hold. His wolf didn't care that Sean had no desire to be alpha or that the official challenge would claim the life of Nic's father if Nicholas Kagan didn't willingly pass the spirit wolf on. It wanted the power the top spot offered. Nothing else mattered.

"I'm newly matured, and I'm horny. I know that's normal, but every unmated female I come across stirs me. I don't know if my interest is purely physical or if, subconsciously, I'm shopping for a mate." Because without a mate to birth him an heir, he'd never be able to hold on to the alpha spot.

Noah dropped his hand. "Stop fighting your wolf and trust yourself. That's the best advice I can give. There're no guarantees in life or in love. Remember that. You make a choice, then live with it."

Sean raised a brow. "Speaking from experience?"

"Yeah." Noah spun on his heel and walked toward the door. "Call if you need me. It's not like I have anything better to do with my life."

The front door banged shut behind him. Sean stared at it for a minute, then grabbed his wallet. "Well, I do, and it involves me, some whiskey, and maybe a few beers."

And a bar where he'd be sure not to stumble across any shifter females.

CHAPTER TWO

Every female in the bar either sneaked coveted glances at him or openly ogled him. At over six foot with a muscular build, sandy blond hair, and gray eyes, Sean was used to the attention. The full moon's influence doubled his appeal. Whether the humans realized it, they were swayed by the pheromones he gave off. Luckily for him and the women around him, his only goal for the night was to get drunk. The spinning room proved he was well on his way to achieving it.

He drained the last of his whiskey, then slammed the glass down. A fiery burn mapped a path to his gut, numbing him and quieting his wolf. There was a reason some shifters turned into alcoholics. Other than finding one's fated mate—an almost impossible feat—booze was the only thing that gave them peace. Of course, once the buzz wore off, they were back in the same boat—fighting their instincts and hiding their hungers.

The waiter who'd been making regular stops at his table paused in his loop around the bar. "Another?"

"No. A lager." He held up his hand. "Make that two. It'll save you a trip."

The human glanced from the empty glass, Sean's tenth, to his face but didn't comment. Sean had become a regular over the past month, and his tolerance was well known. The waiter nodded, then slipped into the crowd with his tray held high.

Eyes closed, Sean rested his head against the worn vinyl seat and ticked off the minutes until the full moon's peak faded. The one-hour window every month marked the time when destinies could be altered—from changes in alphas to conceptions. Once it passed, the pack's future was locked in place for another month. Only matings could happen anytime. A good thing, according to their elders. A male never knew when he'd meet his mate.

"Here you go." The waiter delivered his bottles.

"Thanks."

Sean grabbed one and drank half before turning his attention to peeling off the label, but paused with the soggy paper between his thumb and forefinger. A sweet scent carried over the stench of sweat and stale beer. Unable to resist, he inhaled. The unmistakable fragrance of an unmated, fertile female filled his lungs.

He cursed, even while his body reacted, and his wolf stirred. Just his luck. He'd escaped the lure of his pack's women by surrounding himself with humans, but hadn't counted on a Tanner female showing up. Why had she? Their lands were thirty minutes away by car, longer in wolf form. He dragged in another lungful. No other shifters accompanied her, either.

A surge of protectiveness tensed his muscles. By herself, she'd draw the attention of all the males in the bar, just as she'd caught his. The humans would hit on her. Touch her.

Seduce her.

Then again, that might be what she wanted. Males weren't the only ones who suffered the effects of the full moon. She probably came shopping for a lover, maybe two. She'd be sensitive, responsive, insatiable. She'd use them all night long until they were too tired to move.

A low growl rumbled in his chest. No. He wouldn't go there. It was none of his business. She had a right to see her needs met any way she wanted.

He chugged his beer, then grabbed the second, but froze with the bottle at his lips. Her gaze bored into him, demanding he acknowledge her. He didn't want a visual to feed his erotic thoughts, but couldn't ignore her pointed gaze.

He glanced at where she stood near the edge of the dance floor. He noted the short skirt she wore and the halter top that barely contained her plump breasts, but didn't let his gaze linger on her lush body. He focused on her face and the clues it offered of her personality. Platinum-blonde hair caressed her shoulders, and gray shadow drew attention to her icy-blue eyes.

His heart stopped.

The strength emanating from her mesmerized him. Part came from the fact that she housed an arctic wolf, one of the rarer varieties. The rest stemmed from her force of will. It burned strongly in her direct stare. She had dominant written all over her. Actually, she could've worn a button that said ALPHA FEMALE IN TRAINING. He could see her ruling a pack at her mate's side...at his side.

He ground his teeth, irritated by his thoughts. It was the same stuff he'd been dealing with for months. He wanted to hate Nic for putting him in the position, but Sean couldn't. He understood his friend's dilemma and his pain. Walking away from Riley had broken Nic. Sean only hoped Nic got himself together soon. The only responsibility Sean wanted was what being the public face of Kagan Industries brought.

The Tanner female licked her lips, a slow swipe of her tongue that Sean followed with his gaze. It was hard not to fall under her spell. He couldn't let it happen, though. He tipped his bottle toward her, then looked away. The dismissal would come off as a slap in the face. It bothered him, but not enough to invite her closer. Sex didn't fit into his schedule for the night, and that was what would happen if he got his hands on her.

He finished his beer, then set to work peeling the label, a habit he'd developed over the past month of drinking alone. She watched him. He didn't need to see her blue eyes to know. His skin tingled and his body tightened. He adjusted himself, but his jeans offered little room for the state she left him in.

The music pumping from the speakers changed from some fast song to a sultry one that encouraged couples to grind against each other. After a moment, the sensation of her gaze faded. Had she accepted an offer to dance? He shouldn't care, but he scanned the dance floor for her. Her blonde hair caught his eye.

The humans near her moved, giving him an unobstructed view. She danced alone, swaying with the music and looking unbelievably hot. He leaned forward and enjoyed the show. It didn't hurt to watch her. The humans around her stopped dancing and focused on her too. If the smile on her face was any sign, she enjoyed their attention.

A human slipped his arm around her waist and pulled her against him. She laughed, and Sean fought the growl threatening to erupt. Intentional or not, she triggered his instincts. He wanted to go to her and rip her away from the human. If the female craved a lover's touch, Sean would be the one to satisfy her, not a man who wouldn't understand the hungers plaguing her.

Sean knew what she craved—a rough encounter that left her begging for more. He'd give it to her. He'd take her out back, push her against the wall, and…

He cursed a second time and shoved from his seat. Gaze locked on the hall leading to the bathrooms, he strode forward. He needed to get himself under control. With twenty minutes left of the full moon's peak, he was too revved to think clearly.

The door smacked closed behind him, and the music cut off. He planted his hands on the counter and hung his head. Deep breaths cleared his lungs of her lingering scent, but the image of her undulating body burned in his mind.

Had he ever seen a more beautiful female? Or met one who so boldly held his gaze, demanding he treat her as his equal?

Sure, there were gorgeous and strong females in his pack. He'd also crossed paths with some humans who fit the description. So what was it about the Tanner female that left him with an undeniable ache and shaky hands?

"You're not getting edgy? Irritable? Or feel like you're going to come out of your skin?" Noah's words repeated in Sean's head.

His pent-up breath escaped in a rush. His stubbornness was the reason behind his fascination, nothing more. The rationalization strengthened him. He'd have to take Noah's advice and trust himself. What better time than the present? He would sit back at his table, finish his drink, and go home. Tomorrow, he'd lock himself in his room and shift. Depending on how easy it was to wrangle control from his wolf, he'd repeat it outside.

With his plan set, he left the men's room. A few feet into the bar, his wolf stirred. Its unease matched Sean's. Something was wrong. A survey of the crowded dance floor told him what—the female was gone. So was the guy who'd had his hands all over her. The obvious assumption was that they'd left together. Sean's gut warned him she was in trouble. He pushed his way through the crowd and bolted out the door.

A man's vehement curse rang out.

Sean followed the sound to the alley. The human from the bar held the Tanner female's hand in a rough grip. Anger thinned his lips. The red splotch on his cheek served as a good indicator of why.

Sean ran forward and grabbed the man's forearm, squeezing hard enough to tear a squeak from him. The moment he released the female, Sean slammed him into the wall. "I don't think the lady wants to leave with you."

"That's none of your business."

Sean raised a brow. "Isn't it?"

"No. It's not."

"Think again. She's mine." The second the words left his mouth,

Sean regretted them. Too late. That was the problem with speaking while his emotions were running high. Stuff got past his internal filter.

"What? Are you her boyfriend or something?"

Sean snorted. "Or something."

"Then you must not be satisfying her. 'Cause she wouldn't have her hand down my pants if you were."

Sean's fangs slid into place, and the tips of his claws pushed against his skin. He closed his eyes in case they started glowing. With his wolf close, Sean didn't trust himself not to lose control. Shifters not only had to remember they were stronger than humans, but they had to maintain a low profile. Only a select few humans in the higher levels of government knew about them, not the public. For their species' sake, it had to stay that way.

He tightened his control over his wolf, reminding it of where they were, then leaned close to the human. "If you want to wake up tomorrow with no broken bones, you best walk away now."

"I should say that to you."

"You wouldn't last thirty seconds against me, buddy."

"I hate cocky bastards. I can—"

"Tell you what. If you want to fight, let's fight. All you have to do is push me away and throw the first punch." Sean moved his hands to the wall on either side of the guy's torso.

The human planted his palms against Sean's chest and shoved, then pushed again and again to move him. The guy cursed before slipping under Sean's arm. "That proves nothing. I can lock my knees too. If I had a better angle, you'd be on the ground."

Sean stood, arms loose at his side. "Well, you're free now. Hit me."

The guy swung. Sean intercepted his fist a moment before the blow connected. He tightened his grip on the guy's knuckles until the human's eyes widened. "You lose. Get out of here, and the next time a woman doesn't like something you say or do, listen to her. Got it?"

"Sure. Whatever."

Sean released him and followed his retreating back with his gaze until the human disappeared around the corner. "Now that he's gone, tell me why you came out alone. That's asking for trouble."

Silence answered him.

Sean pivoted and scanned the empty alley for the Tanner female. She was gone. He jogged to the main road and swept his gaze over the area. Only a few humans lingered on the street. He stood there a moment and debated what to do, then shook his head.

"Not my problem. She's a big girl. If she doesn't want me to protect her, that's her decision." It was also the best one for him. He wanted to wake up alone tomorrow.

CHAPTER THREE

Sean took the long way back to the Kagan Industries office. His intention had been to pass out on the couch in the downstairs office. The Tanner female's intrusion on his night of drinking killed his plans. The buzz he'd developed had morphed into a compulsion he couldn't explain. Every instinct within him demanded he hunt down the female. He just wasn't sure what drove him—physical needs or something more. It was the latter which left him prowling the streets of the humans' town while he sorted out his thoughts.

He'd been dealing with his instincts ever since he matured. Every time he crossed paths with an eligible female, the same scenarios—wondering if she'd be a fitting mate or if genetics would gift them with strong offspring—had dominated his mind. The only difference was that as soon as he got away from whichever woman had caught his eye, the urge to claim her as his mate passed.

But the Tanner female?

He could not stop thinking about her. Even with the full moon's influence fading, the pull to her remained.

Why?

The question repeated in his head. He couldn't figure it out. Sure, she was hot. Getting her naked body under him would leave him sated, but there was more to his fascination. Something about her struck him as different.

Maybe she's my fated mate, and that's why I can't stop thinking about her. He snorted at his thought. He'd have a better chance of getting struck by lightning than finding his fated mate. Actually, that wasn't quite accurate. He very well might cross paths with her. Recognizing her was a different story.

There was no instant sign, but if you were lucky enough to find your fated mate, man and wolf merged, becoming what their gods had intended when they'd created shifters. Too bad their gods didn't have the foresight to clue them in better. Matching tattoos would've been nice. No, the only advice their elders had to give was to mate someone you cared about and hope for the best. If you were lucky, the female you chose was your fated mate. If not, then at least you had a friend to walk through life with.

At the edge of the town park, he hesitated. If he continued past it, he'd reach the Kagans' office in less than five minutes. He could lock himself inside or he could return to the bar and try to pick up the female's scent. It wouldn't hurt to get to know her. The Tanner pack had its issues, including a rotten alpha who didn't deserve the role he held, but not all the Tanner shifters deserved to be shunned, as many of the Kagan pack members had done.

Besides, he still wanted to know why she had been out alone. From what Noah had told him, all unmated females were encouraged to join their monthly mating run—a shifter version of speed dating meant to increase the number of their pack's mated couples.

With his decision made, he cut through the park. Halfway across, he froze. A pair of high heels, along with the top and skirt the Tanner female had worn, were strewn across the grass. He snagged the tattered fabric. She'd shifted on the run, not bothering to undress. Trying to escape someone? Maybe the human from the bar or another shifter male?

His heart rate kicked up, and he scanned the grounds. Nothing moved. A deep breath didn't give him any clues, either. She'd been gone awhile.

He pressed his nose to her shirt and inhaled. Her fragrance seeped into his lungs, giving him the means to track her. He dropped her shirt and ran. It'd be quicker and easier if he let his wolf out, but he couldn't risk it. For one, he didn't know if he'd be able to retake control, but more importantly, if a human spotted a wolf running through town, they'd go for their guns or call the police. Neither would end well. He needed to find her and fast.

The scent of blood drifted to him. He pivoted and followed it. A few hundred feet into the woods, he spotted a tuft of hair. More blood was streaked along a nearby tree. Worry gripped him. The female was running blindly. Fear would do that, except he didn't smell anyone else, not another shifter or human. Whatever set her off had frightened her, though.

A flash of white caught his attention. He turned and collided with her gaze. Sides heaving, she froze and watched him through her wolf's eyes.

"Are you okay?"

Her steady stare answered him. In her animal form, she couldn't speak to him, but she didn't shake her head or nod either.

"Shift and tell me what happened." He took a step toward her. "I can—"

She bolted away from him—straight toward the town's main street.

He did the only thing he could. He opened himself to his wolf and shifted.

CHAPTER FOUR

The Tanner female was fast. Sean had to give her that, but he wanted her safely in his arms before she hurt herself again. He pivoted, sliding on the damp grass, and ran full out to intercept her. She caught sight of him and turned in the opposite direction. He inwardly cursed, but followed, urging her toward the Kagan office.

After several minutes, the pond at the rear of their property came into view, and he calmed. If he could get her to shift, he'd invite her inside and patch up her cuts.

She slowed her frantic pace and came to a stop near the fountain. He sat on his haunches several feet away, giving her enough space so she wouldn't feel trapped, then reached for the tether to his wolf. He gave a rough metaphysical yank on it, but the animal didn't fight him. It slipped into the mystical field where it had lived its entire life and allowed his human shape to reform. The ease with which it retreated shocked him. He wouldn't question it. The female didn't need to know how he struggled with his instincts.

He crouched so as not to appear as threatening and folded his hands loosely in front of him. "Well, now that you made me ruin my clothes and took me for a run through the woods, are you going to tell me what frightened you?"

She stiffened, but didn't shift.

He motioned toward the bar. "Was it that pathetic human? Or a different one, because I'll—"

She shook her head.

"Another shifter, then? Someone from your pack harassing you?" Without the evidence of one, it didn't seem likely, but he couldn't imagine what else would've sent her running.

Again, she shook her head.

"Okay." He waited a moment, then blew out a breath. "Look, why don't you just shift and talk to me? Don't be afraid. I'm not going to hurt you."

A long moment passed while she studied him through her icy wolf's eyes before she eased her tense posture and shifted. He watched in awe as she changed shapes, a sight he'd seen hundreds of times, yet never had the flip in forms mesmerized him the way hers did. For one brief second, a fuzzy image of a white wolf meshed with that of the woman who housed it. A glowing tether connected them, heart to heart. Her wolf's shape faded and hers gained dimension. In the next moment, a naked female stood before him.

Hand planted on her hip, she raised her chin. "I'm not afraid of you."

He swept his gaze over her. It was impossible not to. Full breasts, shapely hips, and lush thighs—she was beautiful. No, gorgeous. Even that description didn't do her justice, but he couldn't think of a better one. He only knew he'd never laid eyes on a more perfect female, but if he didn't tear his gaze from the space between her legs, her opinion of him would be less than stellar.

He glanced into her face. "I'm glad. I didn't want to scare you, but I was afraid someone was after you. When you took off, I reacted. I couldn't let any of the humans see a wolf running through their town."

"You're right." Her shoulders slumped. "I'm sorry. I wasn't thinking."

"Don't apologize. It's the full moon. Makes even the most levelheaded more prone to act on instinct."

"That's what I was trying to avoid by running away from you."

"Me?" He pointed to himself. "What did I do to frighten you? Was it because I shoved that loser against the wall? If so, you should know I didn't hurt him."

"I believe you."

He pushed to his feet. "Then what did I do?"

She skimmed her gaze down his chest to his groin. His body stirred to life under her focused inspection. He tried to will it to behave, but failed miserably. He had the sudden urge to slap his hand over his package. The female was skittish enough. She didn't need to see the evidence of how much he wanted her. Her shaky sigh stopped him.

"Other than looking like a sex god?" She shrugged. "Nothing."

"Sex god?" He grinned, pleased with her description. "Thank you, but why is that a bad thing?"

She ran a hand through her hair. The move lifted her breasts and exposed a cut on her upper arm. The sight of her blood dripping from the wound sickened him. Literally. It wasn't simply empathy or concern for another shifter, but a physical response. His gut rolled.

"—I ran instead."

Her voice registered in his mind, but he didn't catch what she'd said. He shook his head.

"I'm sorry. I drank a lot tonight. The brain's a little sluggish. What did you say?" It was a lie. He wasn't drunk. Even his buzz had worn off, but he didn't want to admit he felt like a failure and a jerk. She'd hurt herself because of *him*.

She gave him a wan smile and approached him, then rose on her tiptoes and laid a hand against his cheek. He gazed into her face from inches away and studied her as the gods had intended her to be. Her makeup had disappeared with her shift. Although artfully done, it hadn't made her prettier. It had merely drawn attention to her features, but it wasn't necessary. Her natural beauty captivated him. He mapped her face with his gaze, searing her image into his memory.

Her short eyelashes were nearly luminescent, and combined with her icy eyes, she appeared ethereal. Her pink lips and flawless skin added to the image. She could've been a snow goddess, but she wasn't cold. The lust displayed on her expression promised a passionate side that could make any male burn. He curled his fist to resist pulling her closer. He wanted her to set him on fire, but listening to her was more important.

"I said"—she dragged her fingertips along his jaw to the corner of his mouth—"I looked at you sitting there all alone, and my possessive instincts flared. I wanted to make you mine, but you dismissed me. I figured you already had a lover, so to avoid humiliating myself, I ran instead."

His first assessment of her had been right. The female was unlike any he'd ever met. It was no wonder he'd been drawn to her. "Do you make a habit of taking what you want?"

"Mmm-hmm." Her eyes twinkled, and her lip quivered. "I'm from the Tanner pack, and we embrace the old ways that say the strong should be rewarded the best prize."

He would've been annoyed by her words if he didn't see the amusement in her gaze. According to the old ways of pack mentality, the weak—whether they were beta shifters or humans—were left to fend for themselves. If they died, then it was nature's way of ridding the pack of the worthless.

Thankfully, the Kagan pack didn't uphold those teachings. If they did, Riley and her twin would've died as infants. Although they ranked as betas in the pack hierarchy, Sean couldn't imagine his life without them.

He settled his hands on her hips. "Is that what I am? A prize?"

"Maybe." She chuckled. "But at the moment, I should say you're my hero. You saved me. I acted like an idiot. What I did was just plain stupid."

"Never use those words to describe yourself. I don't like it." He bent and dragged his parted lips over the delicate column of her neck to the spot right below her ear. "Try words like beautiful, strong, bold, sexy. Those are fitting words for you."

She curled her hand around the back of his head. "And how would you describe yourself?"

He caught her lobe and sucked on it. A shudder ran through her, and she leaned into him, letting him support her weight. "Male."

"Male? That's it?"

"Yes. That covers it. Males aren't special. We just are."

She turned her head, so they were eye to eye. "I beg to differ. You're better than many I know."

"How so?"

"Most of the unmated males from my pack would've been stimulating me by now and making sure I was too aroused to resist them when they pushed me to the ground."

Anger tensed his muscles and tore a low growl from his chest. "That makes them assholes, not males."

She lazily traced his spine. "I agree, which is why I refused to spend my first night as a mature female with them. I figured a one-night stand with a human was better."

"And because of me, you didn't end up with one."

"Another thing I should thank you for. His idea of how we should spend the night involved me tied up with a ball gag in my mouth." She laughed. "As if I would ever submit completely to someone I didn't view as my equal."

Challenge accepted. Except he had a better idea of how to fill her mouth.

"You're welcome, but I am sorry I ruined your night. Will you let me make it up to you?"

She raised a brow. Interest showed in her gaze. "And how do you plan on doing that?"

"I have my ways. Say yes."

She reached between their bodies and brushed her knuckles over his stomach. "Are you sure? Males in my pack have called me demanding and insatiable."

He swung her into his arms. "Females have said the same about me."

A wicked grin spread over her face. "And none were smart enough to claim you?"

He walked toward the patio, then punched in the security code. The door unlocked, and he carried her inside. "Or I was smart enough not to give in to them. It all depends on how you look at it."

She linked her hands behind his neck. "Yes. My answer is yes. I want you to be the first male I make love to as a mature female."

Her answer should've made him happy. Instead, it fed into the possessiveness riding him. Being her first wasn't good enough. He wanted to be her last.

Oh no. Thoughts like that would damn him.

Maybe his offer wasn't the smartest he'd ever made. Too late, though. He never backed down from a challenge. He just needed a moment to get himself together and remember what was at stake.

He set her on her feet away from him, then held out a hand. "I promise to make it memorable, but first, let's patch you up."

"Okay." She twined her fingers with his, and his thoughts scattered.

He inwardly cursed. Get himself together, huh? He'd be lucky if he could slap a couple of bandages on her cuts before he loved her.

CHAPTER FIVE

The female's scent drew Sean closer. Every step from the kitchen to the office where she waited tightened his body and quickened his pulse. He wanted to get drunk on her. Feast on her sweetness. Tease her until she was begging for release.

Make her his.

He shook his head to clear it of the crazy thought. It didn't help. The possessiveness hadn't lessened, no matter how many times he reminded himself he needed to keep it in check.

"Are you going to stand there all night or are you going to"—she grinned—"come over here and see to my needs?"

He loved her assertiveness. He glanced at where she stood near the fireplace. She was tall for a human but average for a female shifter, and the perfect height for him. He could rest his chin on the top of her head and feel her heated breath on his chest. Needing to hold her exactly that way, he placed the items he'd collected on the nearby desk before facing her.

He slipped an arm around her waist and drew her against him. With his cheek pillowed on her silky hair, he asked, "Do you have many?"

"Yes, but I'm confident you'll be able to satisfy me."

So was he. First, he had to tend to her cuts. He released her, then reached for the bandages.

"I don't need anything on them." She twisted her arm, exposing the thin red line. "It's not even bleeding anymore."

"I know." He gently lifted her arm and swabbed an alcohol wipe over her skin. She was right. It wasn't necessary. It didn't stop his desire to tend to her, though. He didn't quite understand why, but wouldn't fight it. What harm did it do to treat her as if she were precious to him? "But you got hurt because of me. It'll make me feel better if I've at least inspected your cuts."

She swallowed hard. "Okay."

Her breathless word made him smile. He finished cleaning the scratch, then dropped to his knees. He focused on her outer thigh to avoid getting distracted by her body. It proved harder than he expected. Breathing in the evidence of her desire left him light-headed and eager.

He laid a hand on her hip to steady himself, then went to work wiping the dried blood from her skin. Much like the one on her arm, the scratch had healed. A bonus of shifter genetics. Although not immortal, they lived hundreds of years compared to the few decades humans did. He swept the square piece of cotton over the pink line once more, then tossed it aside.

He tipped his head back. "Any more?"

Her dilated eyes locked on to his. She shook her head. "No. That's it."

"Good."

He turned his attention to the female in his arms. No hair covered her body. He leaned closer and inhaled, needing to drug himself on her scent. Deep breaths satisfied the craving but made his mouth water. He pressed his lips to her stomach and flicked his tongue out. Her taste hit him. *So good.* She could be his new addiction. He explored her body. Kissed her in all the places that would make her wild. She became his entire focus.

In one quick move, he released her and stood. He captured her mouth with his, swallowing her gasp. For a moment, he wondered if it bothered her he'd explored her body first. Her throaty groan a second later pushed the question aside. She tilted her head and licked the inside of his mouth, an erotic and carnal exploration he was sure he'd never shared with another woman.

He ran his hands over her back, tugging her impossibly closer. Her softness pushed against his chest and her legs tangled with his. She arched into him, and he lifted her, supporting her completely. The small sign of her submission registered in his brain. She trusted him to hold her and not let her fall. Such a little thing; a human wouldn't give it a second thought. A shifter, though? It spoke volumes.

It wasn't quite enough.

He lowered them so they knelt on the soft rug. It took more willpower than he wanted to admit, but he tore his mouth from hers and reached for the soft strip of fabric he'd found in the hall closet. He held it up. "Your turn."

She cocked a brow. "You want me to tie you up?"

"No." He moved behind her and took her wrists, crossing them at the base of her spine. "You will be."

She glanced over her shoulder. "And if I say no?"

He brushed his thumb over the inside of her wrist. "Then we skip this, and I'll lay you down and make love to you."

She licked her lips. "Make it tight. I want to struggle to get my hands on you."

He used the soft fabric to bind her arms, pulling the knot tight, exactly as she'd commanded. His pulse kicked up at the possibilities open to him. He let them skip through his head but focused on the one that left him eager.

He stepped in front of her, and she bent toward him. He stopped her with a hand on her chest. "Wait."

She raised her white-blonde brow again, a gesture he was loving. "Why?"

"I want you to spread your legs wider."

She did. "Like this?"

He loosely wrapped his hand around her throat. "More."

She caught his gaze. Something flashed in her pale eyes. If he didn't know better, he'd call it possession. She closed them and widened her stance until only his hold on her throat held her steady. "Better?"

He rubbed his thumb over her lower lip. "Yes, perfect."

So was she.

He relished the sight of her before him, mouth slightly open and eyes closed, but the need to experience her passion took over.

He brushed his thumb over her lips. "Are you ready to worship me now?"

She peered at him from under hooded eyes. "I don't think eternity would be long enough for that."

For the first time in his life, he was speechless. He swallowed hard.

He gave himself over to the moment. She did as she promised him. She worshipped him. Accepted him. Loved him with her every touch. He wanted to return her devotion—tonight, tomorrow, for an eternity.

Keep her. He wanted to keep her. Make her his.

He dropped to his knees and undid the strap binding her wrists. His hands shook. He ignored the sight, not wanting to think about why they trembled.

The moment she was free, she wrapped her arms around him and kissed him. She ate at his mouth. He let her lead him, enjoying the desperation in her frantic strokes as if she were starved for him, but other desires demanded payment.

His body ached in a way in never had before. She'd ease him, though. Bring him peace. He wanted that—to find heaven in her arms. She was the only one who could give it to him too. The certainty of his thoughts gripped him. No other female would fit him the way she did. If he let her go, another male might steal her from him and mate her. Sean would lose everything.

He tore his mouth from hers.

"I want to own you." He whispered the confession. Crazy or not, the claim felt right.

"Own me how?"

"Keep you. Mate you. Love you from now until the spirit wolf calls us home." He breathed his vow against her ear. "Tell me you want that."

"Yes, I want that." Her voice cracked. "I want to call you my mate. I want that more than anything."

"Oh, baby." He slipped his tongue between her lips and kissed her.

Heaven. She was his heaven.

The knowledge came and went. Primal demands took over. He needed to prove to her she'd made the right choice, that he could satisfy her and be *her* everything. He broke their kiss and let his instincts guide him, loving her until the primitive drive that compelled his vow demanded to be met.

Sean leaned over her and clamped his mouth over her shoulder, biting her. Her soul opened to him. Bright and pure, she was beautiful.

He moved through her and left a piece of his soul behind. It tied him to her. She'd feel him—his needs, his moods, his pain—and be able to comfort him. He wanted to do the same. It would be easy enough. He'd just have to claim a piece of her soul. They would be soul-bonded; joined in life and death. He'd never be separated from her. It was the ultimate act of love, but… He hadn't asked her if she wanted that. He'd asked her to be his mate, not his eternal partner. They were two entirely different things.

No. It wasn't right to take the choice out of her hands. They had a lifetime ahead of them to decide.

He let the piece of her soul he held slip through his fingers. It pained him, but it was the right thing to do. Slow swipes of his tongue eased any pain his bite had caused and sealed his scent into her body, so anyone who got close to her would know she belonged to him.

"My mate." He rested his cheek over his bite mark, a beautiful scar she'd carry for the rest of her life. "Thank you."

He wasn't sure what he was thanking her for—mating him, accepting him, taking a chance on him. He was just glad she had.

CHAPTER SIX

Sean woke to the rhythmic thump of a heartbeat under his ear. He opened his eyes. Strands of pale blonde hair caressing the scarred impression of his teeth filled his vision. Memories returned in a rush. He'd taken a mate—a gorgeous, strong female from the Tanner pack named…

Curses whipped through his head. He didn't know the name of his mate. How ridiculous was that? He'd mated a stranger.

She stirred. A smile graced her lips. "Mmmm…good morning, mate."

Did she even know his name? Did she care? His heart rate quickened. What had he done? Made the biggest mistake of his life. That was what.

He scrambled back and crouched several feet away. She propped on her elbow. The warmth in her expression faded. An icy indifference replaced it. No doubt his reaction caused her mood change. Why wouldn't it? She'd woken happy and in the arms of her mate, and he'd freaked out.

"I didn't mean to react that way. It's just that I…" He shoved to his feet and ran a hand through his hair. Deep breaths filled his lungs with his mate's scent, and he calmed. The rapid beat of his heart slowed. Reality returned.

Okay. He took a mate. This was not the end of the world. He was sure she was a very nice female. He hoped. He exhaled roughly. "It's just that the rashness of what we did last night left me a little uneasy this morning. I don't even know your name."

She stood and held out a hand. "My name is Jenna Tanner. Michael Tanner, the alpha of my pack, is my uncle. I hate his guts and pray that one of these full moons, a dominant will be brave enough to challenge him. He needs to die."

Was that why she agreed to mate him? Was she shopping for a male who could offer her the alpha female spot? He snorted. "Well, if you think I can be the one to take him out, you mated the wrong guy. I don't even want to lead my pack, let alone your screwed-up one."

Jenna cringed and dropped her hand. "That's not why I agreed to mate you."

"Then why did you?"

She swept her gaze over him and shook her head. "I have no clue."

"Look. This is not going the way I expected. Why don't I get us some breakfast? Then we can talk."

"Sure."

"Great." He walked toward the hall closet where they kept spare clothes for unexpected shifts. He grabbed a pair of sweats, a T-shirt, and flip-flops. "Make yourself at home. Get a shower or whatever. I'll be back in..." He glanced at the clock. The diner wouldn't open for another hour. The proper thing to do was spend this time getting to know his mate. He slid his gaze back to her. Eyes narrowed and lips pressed in a straight line, she appeared thoroughly ticked off. He couldn't blame her. He'd acted like an ass. Yeah, they both needed a few minutes. "An hour or so. Maybe closer to two. Diner's not the fastest."

Without waiting for a response, he opened the lockbox stashed in the corner of the closet, took a couple of twenties, then slipped out the front door. He needed this time to get his thoughts in order before he ruined his relationship with his only mate.

———

The turtleneck Jenna had found in one of the offices of the Kagan Industries' building clung to her curves, drawing attention to her braless state, and the mesh shorts she'd discovered in another room slid down her hips. At the moment, she didn't care about the ill-fitting or mismatched outfit.

Embarrassment gripped her, leaving Jenna—the top dominant female of the Tanner pack—shaking and fighting tears.

The male she'd mated didn't want her.

She choked on a sob and quickly pressed a hand to her mouth, muffling the sound, then hurried down the street before some well-meaning human approached her. Even with the leave-me-alone expression she wore, humans stared at her. Probably wondering what was wrong with her. Some appeared concerned, others judging. She ignored them. Their opinions didn't matter. They'd never understand what she was going through.

Humans didn't have to follow the same rules shifters did. They didn't have to deal with the instincts of the animal sharing their body. They didn't have to constantly worry about defending their position in the pack. And they didn't have to always appear calm, even when new and unfamiliar emotions left them confused.

Shifters, unfortunately, did have to worry about those things. They had to be strong, mentally and physically, in all situations. If they weren't, they'd dishonor their pack, their ancestors, and their gods. No shifter wanted that. At least no respectable shifter wanted that. Yet here she was, sniffling and huddling in shame, hoping nobody she knew saw her.

She stopped walking and straightened her spine. If this was how she was going to react to a little heartache, she might as well concede her position of dominance and move to the bottom of the pack.

No way.

A couple of deep breaths settled the trembling in her limbs and cleared the lump from her throat. She had to face the facts, not react solely on her emotions as she'd done last night. Listening to her instincts had been an epic failure. Hours after entering into a lifetime bond, her mate had shamed her, scrambling away from her as if she had fleas or some contagious disease. It didn't take a genius to guess why he'd reacted that way.

He regretted mating her.

The lump in her throat returned. So did the pricking in her eyes. She pressed her lips together and took deep, slow breaths until the tears choking her faded.

Her mate's reaction to her was a devastating blow to her self-esteem, but it wasn't the end of the world.

It only felt like it.

Jenna scrubbed her hands over her face. She did not need a male in her life. She especially did not need a mate who hadn't cared enough to ask her name before mating her. Or where she lived. Or even her cell number. Then again, basic manners hadn't been important then. Lust had ruled him.

She sighed. There was no denying it. He'd acted on his instincts too, and once he came to his senses, he'd make the most of the situation, just as she was trying to do. If she had to guess, it wouldn't take him long to reach the best outcome...for him. She was powerful. Any children she had would be too.

A growl threatened to escape. She tightened her control over her primal side. With humans close by, she couldn't afford the slip. Her restraint didn't kill the disgust choking her, however. She'd seen firsthand how a breeding relationship could hurt a woman. Shame her. Make her feel as if she were nothing more than an incubator.

Her best friend, Mya, was stuck in one of those degrading relationships, and she had no way out of it. Her mate had knocked her up, then ordered Mya off their pack lands once he learned the sex of the babies she'd conceived. He had no use for girls and didn't want to have to support them. So Mya had left. She'd had no choice but to obey her mate.

Actually, Mya's was probably an extreme case. Still, it reminded Jenna of what was at stake. Her pride. Her future. And her sanity.

She would rather live out her life alone than be a breeding partner.

Jenna waited until the street was empty before hurrying across it. If she was lucky, her wallet, keys, and phone would still be under the bush she'd stashed them last night. She wanted to be out of this town before her mate came looking for her.

If he even bothered.

———

The front door was locked when Sean returned. Trepidation tightened his muscles, but he entered the code and opened the door. Silence greeted him.

"Jenna!"

No answer.

He set the two coffees and bag of donuts on the hall table and rushed into the office. Empty. The why was obvious—she left. Still, he went through the extensive building, opening every door and calling out to her.

His steps dragged by the time he returned to the office. He leaned against the doorframe and stared at the spot where he and Jenna had made love. The memory washed over him, and the same rightness he'd felt in her arms the night before returned. His wolf hadn't fought him while he'd mated her. It hadn't encouraged him either. It had remained silent, much as it had been all morning. No help there.

"Trust my instincts, huh?" Noah had told him that. He'd also said that you make a choice then live with it.

"Well, I made mine—Jenna Tanner." And he wouldn't give up on her or them.

He grabbed his cell phone from where he'd left it on the desk the night before and dialed Noah's number.

"Hello?" Noah's gruff voice filled the line.

"What can you tell me about Jenna Tanner?"

"Why do you want to know?"

The protective edge to Noah's voice brought a smile to Sean's lips.

"Because I mated her last night, and I didn't handle the morning after too well. She took off, and I know nothing about her other than her name."

Noah laughed. "Wow. I don't even know what to say."

"Start with congratulations, then tell me where I can find my mate."

"Congratulations." The sincerity in Noah's voice rang true. "Jenna is a wonderful female. You couldn't have picked a better mate."

"Thanks." He grinned. "I agree. She's perfect, but I really messed up. I'm worried she thinks I regret mating her."

"Do you?"

"No, but I rushed into it. I should've waited until I got to know her better."

"Can't argue that, but you have plenty of time to do so now."

"True, and I'm going to make sure I do it right this time." Sean rubbed at the back of his neck. "And I don't think she's going to want to live with my parents or little brothers while we get to know each other."

"Doubt it."

He needed a house. Maybe a ring. He wanted to be married and have their union blessed under the light of the moon before they took their relationship to the next step. No way did he want to get her pregnant without the official documents that told the world she was his.

He snagged his keys. "Look, I've got stuff to do for Jenna. I want her happy. So, tell me where I can find her."

"She lives in a blue trailer about a mile from my house. You can't miss it. It's the only one with a vegetable garden in the front yard."

Then he'd make sure their house had one. "Great. Talk to you later."

Sean ended the call and rushed to the door. He had a lot of planning ahead of him. No way did he want to mess up their second meeting. A woman like Jenna would only give him one chance to right his wrong.

CHAPTER SEVEN

The sound of the front door opening sped Jenna's pulse.

Her mate had come to her.

Jenna turned off the water in the sink, dried her hands, and ran from the kitchen to the living room. Her heart sank at the sight of Noah's signature dark blond ponytail.

Noah turned at her approach, revealing a huge potted container overflowing with flowers. Fat yellow chrysanthemums rose above a bed of delicate white mums. The contrast of size and color was striking, but Noah would know that. The hardened dominant who should've been leading her pack instead of her uncle had a soft spot for flowers. Noah had turned his dead mate's love of gardening into a successful business.

Jenna froze, knowing if Noah got any closer he'd be able to scent Sean on her. Her mate had laved the bite on her shoulder, ensuring his smell would remain a part of her for the rest of her life and warning all other males away from her. "What are you doing here?"

"I came to offer my congratulations."

Shoulders slumping, she linked her hands in front of her. "You know."

Although she couldn't hide her mating forever, she wasn't ready to face the realities of her mated status. Or that her mate had yet to seek her out. He might not know where she lived, but Noah spoke to his cousin who was a Kagan pack member. Word might've gotten around. The Kagan pack was a close-knit group.

Actually, when she thought of it that way, it made perfect sense Noah would come here. Who better to share her mate's regret than Noah, a member of her pack Jenna respected? She'd never take her anger out on him, especially when he stood in front of her with a warm smile on his face. Noah rarely wore one, except in the presence of his friend Ethan.

Noah set the potted container on the coffee table, clearing magazines and newspapers to make room for the huge display. "Sean Reynolds called me right after he discovered you ran out on him."

Sean Reynolds. Top dominant of the Kagan pack and the male rumored to be the next in line to be alpha since the alpha's son had left the pack. The Tanner males didn't like that rumor. Not one little bit. Sean was strong. Very strong. And he'd made it clear he didn't like how Michael Tanner led his pack.

Nerves and excitement warred within her, leaving a tremor in her hands. The rest of Noah's statement kept the emotions at bay.

"I didn't run out. I—" She clamped her mouth shut. Running out was exactly what she'd done.

"What did you do then?" Noah's pointed look demanded she tell him everything.

"He hightailed it out of there first." Jenna took off her apron, balled it, and tossed the worn material at the nearest chair. "I don't think I've ever seen a man move so fast when his life wasn't on the line."

Noah shrugged. "Sean mentioned he didn't handle the morning after too well."

"Didn't handle." Jenna bit the words out. "He made some excuse about the diner being busy in the morning and he wouldn't be back for an hour, maybe two. Two hours, Noah. To get takeout. That was *after* scrambling away from me with a look of terror on his face. Like I was prettier when he was wearing his beer goggles or something."

"Beer goggles?" Noah raised a brow.

Jenna ran her fingers through her tangled hair. It was a good thing Noah had shown up and not Sean. She looked frightful after having baked all morning. She'd needed to do something, though. If she hadn't committed to making a few dozen cookies, she might've driven out to the Kagan pack lands. "Yeah. He was drunk when I ran into him at the bar."

"What about when he mated you?"

Closing her eyes, she let the memory from a few nights ago return. Finally, she sighed. "No. Neither of us were drunk. It just sorta happened, I guess."

Noah studied her for a long moment. He cracked his jaw. "Sorta happened. Care to explain that?"

She forced a laugh. "You were mated. You know how it happens."

Noah took a step forward. His nostrils flared. "Did he ask you? Or simply claim you?"

Jenna covered her mouth to hide her smile. Sean had intrigued her the moment he asked her permission to tend her cuts, but when he'd asked her to mate him, she'd fallen under his spell. She would've agreed to anything. Even soul-bonding.

Noah took another step. "This isn't funny, Jenna. While I can't change what happened, I can make sure Sean understands he should never take another choice from you. Our pride might follow the old ways, but I don't want that for you."

Noah's concern warmed her. She went to him and rested her fingers against his bicep. "Sean asked me. I said yes. There's no need to go all protective of me."

He tucked her hair behind her ear. "Yes, there is. Nobody else will go to bat for you."

She turned away before Noah saw how much those words affected her, making her feel important to someone, even if it wasn't her mate who cared.

The flowers Noah had brought drew her attention. She motioned to the container. "This is beautiful. Thank you."

Noah turned the pot as if looking for the best angle. In truth, the uniform display was perfect. "I woke up early in the year with this combination of flowers in my mind. I knew it'd be beautiful, but I kept finding excuses for not putting it out for sale at the shop. The moment I got Sean's call, I knew why. I was meant to grow this for you."

While Jenna loved flowers, she didn't understand the significance behind them. She was guessing this is where Noah was taking this conversation. "For me?"

"And Sean." Noah caressed one of the yellow flowers. "He's the hope of his pack." Then Noah brushed his forefinger over the smaller white petals. "And you are the goodness of ours. Together, you can lead us into a bright future."

This time, her laugh didn't carry a fake ring to it. Her amusement was genuine. "Nope. According to Sean, he doesn't want to lead his pack, let alone our messed-up one, which is perfectly fine with me. I wasn't meant to be an alpha female."

"And I wasn't meant to be a widower." Noah's stare drove his point home. "But life happens, doesn't it?"

The tightness in her throat made it hard to swallow. She glanced at the floor.

Noah tipped up her chin. "Don't let a chance at love slip through your fingers."

The pain in Noah's eyes broke her heart. Jenna wanted to tell him she wouldn't lose her chance, but she refused to lie to the one pack member who'd always told it to her like it was. "It takes two to make love work. I can't do it alone, and if you haven't noticed, my mate isn't here."

"Sean hasn't abandoned you, Jenna. Give him time to wrap his head around the idea of being a mated male."

"It's been three days." The longest three days of her life.

"If the goddesses bless you the way I think they have, you'll have

Sean by your side for several centuries. A few days now won't matter."

Jenna wanted to wrap Noah's words around her. While she didn't *need* a man in her life, what she'd felt in Sean's arms had been magical. A glimpse of happiness wasn't enough. She wanted centuries of it, exactly as Noah hinted at, but she also loved herself enough not to grovel.

She snatched the balled-up apron and motioned to the kitchen. "Are you hungry?"

Noah shook his head on a sigh, as if understanding her question was meant as a diversion, then raised his gaze to hers. "What kind did you make?"

"Chocolate chip." Lots and lots of chocolate chip cookies. She'd embraced the recipe, knowing she wouldn't have to think about the mechanics of baking. She'd made them hundreds of times before. Her body knew the steps by heart.

"That's Sean's favorite."

Hers too. She tucked the other side of her hair behind her ears. "Maybe there will be some left for him."

"Or maybe he can bake the next batch with you."

Smiling at the thought of the impressive male she'd mated working beside her in the kitchen, Jenna shrugged. "Maybe."

The future was full of maybes. The biggest one at the moment involved the motives of a man she knew little about. All she had to go on was what her heart was telling her. Except, if she listened to those instincts, she'd be driving over to the Kagan pack lands with a plate of cookies. And that might send Sean running a second time.

CHAPTER EIGHT

The sunlight brightening Jenna's bedroom did little to improve her mood. A week had passed since her mate had run from her, claiming he was getting them breakfast. She wouldn't know what he ever returned with since she'd hightailed it out of there too, but there was one thing she was positive about.

Sean Reynolds, her mate and the top dominant of the Kagan pack, hadn't come looking for her. And she hadn't been able to leave town, ensuring he couldn't find her. The longing to return to him had stopped her.

Jenna pressed her forehead to the glass windowpane and fought her tears. She would not cry. She'd managed not to shed a single tear all week, even at night when she'd reached for her mate and only cold sheets had met her touch.

Anger was better.

Screw Sean Reynolds. She'd given him a week. If he didn't want her, she wasn't going to sit around any longer, feeling sorry for herself, or stand by this stupid window for hours on end, wondering if he was going to show. She could survive on her own, exactly like Mya did.

Jenna did not need a male in her life, especially a tall, incredibly handsome Kagan male who made her heart race just thinking about him.

With her head held high, she shoved from her spot by the window and strode across the room. It was time to make some decisions. The first one would be a no-brainer. She couldn't remain on Tanner pack lands. After missing last month's celebrations, she'd be expected to take part in this month's activities. Maybe even join the mating run. Only her neighbor Noah, who'd stopped by earlier in the week to offer his congratulations, knew of her mated status. She'd avoided everyone, friends and family alike.

No more. She was done.

She snatched her cell phone, selected Mya's number from contacts, and dialed. The sound of screaming toddlers filled the line. Jenna grimaced and eased the phone from her ear. After a moment, a door slammed, cutting off the sound of their cries, but stirring Jenna's protective instincts. Why were Mya's girls crying?

"Hello?" Mya's breathless, ragged voice filled the line.

"It's Jenna. Are the twins okay?" As a single mom who no longer lived on pack lands, Mya didn't have the same support network mothers in the pack had.

"Yes. They're fine." Mya lowered her voice. "Todd is here."

Jenna tightened her grip on the phone and fought her anger. "Did your loser mate finally decide to meet his kids?"

"Leave it alone, Jenna."

"Your happiness and the twin's safety are my business. I'm your friend."

"I know you are. I'm grateful for that. Other than the humans I work with, you're the only person on my side, but this is none of your business."

"Call the human cops on him, and while they have him locked up for the night—"

"Stop." Mya sighed. "As their dad, he has a right to see them, and as my mate, he has a right to see me. Mating law guarantees him those things. It doesn't require him to support us, protect us, or even be nice to us. Todd says he's had a change of heart, though. He thinks he's ready to be a dad and wants to spend time with us."

A snarky comment sat on the tip of her tongue, but Jenna clamped her mouth shut before she said anything to upset Mya. It wouldn't change anything. Female shifters had no rights, unless their mates or guardians granted them.

Jenna worked her jaw, easing the pressure. "Do you think he's sincere?"

"No." Mya snorted. "I'm going to be coming into heat next month. He's here for sex."

Squeezing the bridge of her nose, Jenna fought her frustration. "He kicked you out because you got pregnant. Why would he be sniffing around you now? Does he want more kids he can abandon? And how are you going to feed and—"

"I have a job now and a decent apartment. I'm doing fine. I don't need Todd. Besides, I won't get pregnant. He brought condoms, even wrapped them up as a gift and handed them to me with a smile on his face."

If she could, Jenna would rip Todd's throat out, but as one of Michael Tanner's loyal dominants, doing so would only end Jenna's life. Michael believed wholeheartedly in revenge.

"Where did you get a job?" Jenna asked to change the subject. As much as Mya's situation infuriated Jenna, there wasn't a lot that could be done about it. At least not while Todd lived.

"The Black Widow. It's a bar in one of the human towns nearby. I'm waiting tables. It's tiring, but I'm getting a dollar above minimum wage, and I get to keep my tips, not share them with the rest of the staff. Plus, my boss is always stopping by with groceries, and the other waitresses take turns watching the twins when I'm working. For free too. Can you believe it? They do it out of the goodness of their hearts."

"Really?" The humans Jenna had interacted with seemed cold and self-centered. Of course, her only interactions with them were at the college where she was taking nursing courses, and admittedly, she'd stuck to casual conversations only. Befriending humans could be dangerous. They might learn something they shouldn't.

"I know what you're thinking, but they're good humans. They make me laugh. They look out for us. Make us feel as though we're family." Mya chuckled. "They're like my own personal pack."

Jenna smiled and some of her tension eased with the warmth in her friend's voice. Mya trusted these people. That much was clear. "Do you think they need another waitress? I'm looking to get something part-time." She'd need the extra money. The hand-me-down trailer she lived in was rent free, thanks to Noah. Once she left the pack, she'd have to pay for a place.

"You want to be a waitress? I thought you were thinking about asking Michael if you could reopen the clinic once you graduate?"

"No. I'm going to ask him if I can leave the pack for a while."

Silence stretched. Finally, Mya asked, "What happened?"

"I mated a stranger a week ago, then he promptly took off. Haven't seen him since."

"Oh no!" Mya gasped. "Are you okay?"

Eyes burning, she reached for the crumpled photo Noah had given her. She smoothed the wrinkles out, glad she hadn't torn the thing in a fit of frustration, and stared at Sean's face. Contentment slipped through her, even as she fought the sense of peace looking at his image brought. She didn't want to feel any soft emotions toward her no-show mate. It was hard not to, though. He was a part of her. She felt his emotions, his drivers, and his goodness. The warmth and brightness of his soul radiated through her.

Why hadn't he come to her? Or more to the point, why hadn't she gone to him?

She pressed his picture to her chest. They needed to talk. Neither of them had planned this. Maybe they could date. Or at least become friends. She didn't want to end up like Mya, who hated her mate.

"Yeah." Jenna nodded, even though Mya couldn't see her. Doing so made Jenna feel more confident. "I am. It was kinda a spur-of-the-moment thing. We're both still finding our way. In the meantime, I need to be off our pack lands before the next full moon. I don't want Michael finding out who I mated."

"So you didn't mate one of our males?"

"No." Jenna rolled her eyes. She would've rather remained unmated. Most of their males were jerks, like Todd, or beaten down and too afraid to challenge their alpha. "I mated a male from the Kagan pack."

"Oh, my! Aren't you lucky for snagging one of them? I hear they're good in—" Mya gasped. "Todd!"

Static filled the line, along with the whimpering of Mya's little girls. Then a male's voice boomed, drowning out the girls' cries. "I'm glad I stood by this door so these little brats could hear their mama. I must agree with my breeder, though. You *are* lucky for snagging a Kagan. Our alpha will be pleased. He's wanted his hand in the Kagan pack for years. With you as the alpha's mate, he'll have that. I'm sure that was your plan all along, right?"

"I don't even want to lead my pack, let alone your screwed-up one." Sean's words skipped through Jenna's head.

Sweat trickled down her spine. Her mate didn't want to be alpha. She couldn't imagine why. He was powerful and pure. His goodness brightened her soul. Whatever the reason, though, she'd rather run to the other side of the country, never getting the chance to reconnect with Sean and see if they could work out their problems, then force him to do something he didn't want to do.

"No." She shook her head. "I can't do that. Sean's not strong enough." The lie rushed out.

Todd laughed. "Don't lie. I've met Sean many times. He's powerful."

Caught. She licked her lips and tried to come up with a believable diversion. All she had was the truth. "Powerful he might be, but he doesn't want me. I was a mistake. Why do you think he hasn't been around? He mated me a week ago."

"Poor, naïve Jenna. Don't you understand? He doesn't have to *want* you. He just needs to sleep with you every full moon until you conceive a son. That's all I want from Mya, and once I have my boy, I'll let her go to live whatever kind of life she wants with our girls. I have lovers in the pack who satisfy me much better. Too bad none of those females are strong enough to birth me a worthy heir."

Jenna's heart broke for her friend. Mya deserved someone who'd love her and respect her, but as Mya had often said, it was none of Jenna's business, and Todd had mating law on his side. Until he died, she was stuck with him.

"I can't force him." Jenna gave the only response she could.

"Of course not. If you could, I'd lose all respect for Sean. But I'm confident in your ability to seduce him. Once you get him hooked on sex, you can plant the idea in his head. It won't take more than that, I'm sure. Now, if you'll excuse me, I've played daddy enough for today. It's time I act like a real male and call our alpha. We have business to discuss."

Likely which one of her family members would die if she didn't do her part to secure Michael Tanner's hold over Sean's pack? It wouldn't be the first time innocents lost their lives to ensure Michael got his way.

She breathed slowly and carefully to keep her voice calm. "Of course. Will you put Mya back on?"

"Sure. I bet she's eager to finish her conversation with you."

Several moments passed with only Mya's breathing filling the line before she said, "I'm sorry, Jenna. I should've realized something was up when the girls stopped crying."

"Don't be sorry. The truth was bound to come out." It would've been nice if she'd been off Tanner pack lands by then, but such was life. She'd deal with it. Too bad she hadn't dealt with her fate sooner. If she hadn't run from Sean, things might've turned out differently. "I'm more worried about you. Are you okay? The things Todd said —"

"Weren't new. He's made it very clear where I stand and what purpose I serve. Many times. It doesn't bother me anymore, and once I save enough money, the girls and I are out of here."

"Let me help you. I have some money saved and—"

"No." The word dropped harshly between them. "I love you, Jenna. You're my best friend, but I will stand on my own. My girls will learn that being female is not a weakness. I want them to be proud of who they are."

Jenna smiled. Her friend had the strongest inner will of anyone she'd ever known. When Mya said she was going to stand on her own, she meant it. "Okay, but you call me for anything. Do you understand? If you run out of diapers in the middle of the night or one of the girls is sick, you call me. I'll drop everything and rush over. No questions asked."

"Got it."

"Good, because…" The beeping of her phone, indicating an incoming call, tensed Jenna's muscles. She glanced at the display and groaned. "I have to go. Michael's calling me."

"Okay. Talk soon." Mya ended the call.

Unable to delay the inevitable, Jenna answered. "Hello, Michael."

"Jenna, my sweet niece, I hear congratulations are in order."

She cringed at the fake sincerity in her alpha's voice. "Thank you, I—"

"You should've told me immediately about your mating. Hearing from another source makes me look weak."

He was weak. Only fear kept his pack from revolting. She pushed her loathing aside and gave the apology expected of her. "I'm sorry. I was embarrassed when my mate dismissed me."

"And rightly so. You should be ashamed of yourself. I fully expect you to correct this situation and get in your mate's good graces. And once you are, you know what to do."

Her stomach knotted with the sense of trepidation settling over her, but she couldn't avoid Michael's statement. "Yes, I know. You want me to be the alpha female of Sean's pack." So Michael could control it through her.

"Exactly. You are a smart girl." Michael's fake praise made the roiling in her stomach worse. "Now, while you're off securing your position as alpha female, I will keep watch over our younger cousin, Ben. I know how much he means to you, and I'd hate for anything bad to happen to him while you're gone."

Jenna covered her mouth to stop her gasp. Michael would eliminate his own flesh and blood in order to force her compliance. The hatred she held for her alpha burned a little stronger. The worst part was knowing she couldn't do anything about it. Sean didn't want to be alpha to his pack or hers.

"It might take me years to conceive a child. Sean won't even attempt to take over until he has an heir. He needs one beforehand. The magic of the transfer won't guarantee us a child, since he's already mated to me. And you know a baby will make the transition smoother, especially if I conceive a son. He'll want that. He doesn't want to cause any more discontent than he already will be by killing his alpha. Sean is—"

"Stop rambling and explaining things to me I already know." Michael chastised her. "You must work on keeping your moods in check if you expect to be an alpha female. Even my mate can do this."

Her jaw hurt from clenching it. If Michael were here, she'd attack him for his attitude. Consequences be damned. She took a deep breath, burying her fear for Ben and her revulsion for Michael, and straightened her spine. "You're right. It's a skill I must work on. As I said, this week has been hard."

"Don't expect it to get any easier. I want you off Tanner pack lands by sunset."

"You're kicking me out?" She wasn't sure why she asked. Leaving had been her goal.

"Yes. You're no longer a Tanner. You're a Kagan." Michael chuckled. "But don't forget that Ben is a Tanner. He'll always be a Tanner."

Her blood went cold. Ben's face flashed before her eyes. Orphaned as a baby, he'd been raised by their elderly aunt. He was sweet, kind, and nowhere strong enough to fight for himself. "I understand."

"Good, then gather your belongings and get out. Oh, and Jenna?"

"Yes?"

"If you take too long securing the alpha position, I'll send someone else to do so. The Kagan alpha won't live another decade. I promise you that."

Michael ended the call, and she was left debating her options. There was only one to make. She was going to stand on her own two feet, exactly as Mya was doing. Then Jenna would call Sean and tell him everything. After that? She had no clue. It all depended on Sean and what kind of relationship he wanted with her.

CHAPTER NINE

The large house looming before him could've been a second childhood home. Sean had spent many days at his alpha's place, hanging with his best friend, Nic. He'd always felt welcome here. At least he had before Nic skipped town. Sean had avoided his alpha and this home since. He hadn't wanted any of his pack mates wondering about his intentions.

His avoidance had done little to squelch the rumors, though. Everyone kept asking him what his plans were without Nic here. Would he take out Nic's dad? Nicholas Kagan was the oldest alpha in the States, and he was getting weak. Even Sean had sensed that. After five hundred years, it was expected, though. Unlike the immortal Royal shifters, single shifters aged.

Those pack members who'd approached Sean reasoned that if they had to lose their alpha, they wanted the most revered role in the pack to go to someone they knew and trusted. Until a few months ago, that had been Nic. As the alpha's son, it was his right to take his father's place. Nic wasn't here, though. Sean was, and he'd just been ordered to report to his alpha's home…to talk about things.

Sean rolled his shoulders. The tightness in his muscles didn't ease, though. He had a bad feeling about this visit. Until today's abrupt phone call, ordering Sean here, Nicholas had avoided Sean too. There was no evading this meeting, however. When an alpha commanded, his pack obeyed.

With apprehension weighing him down, he climbed the steps to the house, crossed the porch, and slipped inside. The alpha's home was never locked. Any member of the pack could come in, day or night, whether or not they were invited. That was standard practice in most packs. Sean had never felt uncomfortable walking into his alpha's home. Today he did. He stood in the entryway, unsure of his welcome, even though he'd been invited here.

"I'm in the kitchen." Nicholas Kagan's voiced boomed through the home.

Sean forced his feet to move. The refreshing smell of coffee greeted him the moment he stepped into the large kitchen.

Nicholas Kagan, the male who'd acted as a second father to Sean, poured coffee into two mugs, then leaned against the counter. No white or gray streaked his sandy blonde hair. Only the lines on his face outwardly reflected his age, but Sean sensed his alpha's waning strength. Tiredness clung to Nicholas Kagan, making him feel weaker than he had before Nic left.

"Just in time. Coffee's ready. Grab a mug. Creamer's in the fridge. Sugar's in the bowl." With his order given, Nicholas ambled across the room and slipped onto the deck, leaving the sliding glass door open. Apparently, they'd be having this conversation outside in view of the pack's ceremonial circle, where weddings, challenges, and transfers of power occurred.

Great. Just what Sean wanted, to be reminded of the open position in the pack. Except since mating Jenna, he hadn't been overwhelmed with the urge to assert himself in the pack and claim the spot. The only thing dominating Sean's mind was the desire to love his mate again. Of course, that might change once he stood within view of the ceremonial circle, but in this instance, he wanted

Jenna. He missed her. Not for much longer, though. Tonight, he was bringing her home.

He couldn't wait.

Sean pushed aside the thoughts of worshiping his mate and focused on the issues at hand. Nicholas had invited him here to talk. Sean snagged the mug, skipping the creamer and sugar, and followed his alpha outside. The sooner this conversation was over, the sooner he could go to Jenna.

He took up a position next to Nicholas at the railing, propping his elbows on the wood, and surveyed the land from the same viewpoint his alpha did every morning. The open back yard had a couple of birdbaths and benches, along with a rose garden that had been planted by their late alpha female. No doubt about it. This secluded spot was serene, inviting, and fitting for the alpha of the pack.

Sean waited for the compulsion that had plagued him for months to seize him, demanding he claim this home, along with the title of alpha. The primal drive didn't choke him. Or even tease him with promises of power. Nor did his wolf urge Sean to cross the backyard and climb the hill to the ceremonial circle. It had no desire to go there either. It wanted to return to their female.

There was only one conclusion he could make—Jenna had tamed him.

The tension in his shoulders eased. It was good to be in charge again. Fighting with his baser half was draining. He took a sip of his coffee. "Why did you call me here?"

"The Shifter Council has invited me to bring my son to the next meeting since he wasn't able to attend the last one."

"And you want me to contact him for you?"

"No." Nicholas set his mug on the railing and turned to Sean. "I want you to go in his place."

Sean stared at his alpha, unsure of what to say. He hadn't been expecting this.

Nicholas chuckled. "Catch you off guard?"

"Yes." Sean placed his mug behind him and studied his alpha. The neutral expression he wore didn't offer any clues as to his motive. "Why do you want me to go? I'm not next in line to be alpha."

"No, but my son's not here, and my daughter is too young to be entertaining any ideas of mating a male who can take the spirit wolf from me."

About four years too young. Hannah, Nic's sister, was still considered an immature youth, even though she'd soon start shifting. Female shifters developed that ability before males as a protective mechanism. Sean hated knowing their females had to defend themselves.

Jenna's explanation of why she hadn't wanted to remain on her pack lands for her first night as a mature shifter returned. The Tanner males took what they wanted, when they wanted it. And he'd allowed his mate to return to the Tanner pack lands. Only knowing Noah was watching over her in Sean's absence stopped his worry from consuming him. Still, it wasn't right. Jenna belonged with him. Tonight, he'd fix his mistake in letting her go.

"I don't want to be alpha." For the first time, neither did his wolf. Thanks to Jenna.

"Yeah?" Nicholas narrowed his eyes. "Since when? Soon as my son left, the rumors started. Heard you were going to challenge me. Figured I'd save you the trouble."

For a second time in a matter of minutes, Sean stared at his alpha. Commonsense cut through the shock. Nicholas had asked a question. It demanded an answer. "Since I took a mate. Now all I want to do is worship her."

"Congratulations." Nicholas smiled, warmth replacing his normal indifference. "Who's the lucky female?"

"Jenna Tanner." Sean gripped the railing. If Nicholas had something disparaging to say about Jenna because of her birth pack, Sean was going to have a hard time resisting the urge to attack him for it.

Nicholas glanced from where Sean's fingers were wrapped

around the wooden railing to Sean's face. Nicholas's grin widened. "Protective, much?"

"A bit." Sean forced his fingers to unclench. Going by his alpha's reaction, Nicholas didn't have a problem with Sean's choice. "Tanners aren't exactly liked around here."

"As long as she doesn't cause issues among the pack and treats you right, I couldn't care less what pack she came from. Same goes for any member of the pack who takes an outsider as a mate." Nicholas picked up his coffee and turned his attention to the yard. "Now, answer my question. Will you be attending the Shifter Council meeting with me or not?"

His alpha's response eased the last bit of apprehension Sean held, but it didn't change his stance. "As I said, I have no intention of being alpha. That's Nic's fate."

"And again, Nic isn't here." Nicholas shot him a hard glare. "He abandoned us and left our pack open for an outsider to take it over. Or worse, he paved the way for our dominants to fight among themselves to move up in rank, maybe even think about challenging me. I can't allow that to happen. None of our males are strong enough to protect our pack. I won't be able to let them claim the spirit wolf. I'll have to kill them."

"But you think I'm strong enough."

"I know you are, and if my son is too weak to step up and claim his fate, you will take it."

Sean turned his attention to his coffee while he worked through his thoughts. He took small sips until he'd drained the cup, then set it aside. "Nic will claim his position in the pack when he's ready. He's got to work through some stuff."

"And while he's off playing human or doing whatever he's doing, the pack is going to shit. Our pack mates need the security of knowing that when the time comes, a strong, capable male will fill my shoes."

Sean shook his head. He understood what his alpha was saying, but he couldn't get past one point. "This is Nic's fate. I don't want to steal it from him. Once he gets himself together and returns home, he'll want to reclaim his pack. I can't guarantee my wolf will give up the spirit wolf willingly. If it doesn't, I don't want to stand in our sacred circle with my best friend, knowing one of us will die."

Nicholas hung his head. "He won't tell me why he left."

Sean wouldn't be divulging the information either. He'd made a promise to Nic to keep his secret. Sean wouldn't break it, but there was one thing he could do. "Yes. I will go to the Shifter Council meeting with you and act as the next in line here at home, but once Nic returns, I'll step aside. That's the best I can do."

After a long moment, Nicholas sighed. "We leave in four days. Use that time with your mate wisely."

"I plan on it." As long as Jenna didn't lunge for his throat, the next time, she saw him.

CHAPTER TEN

Sean had no trouble finding Jenna's home later that day. While obviously old, the trailer appeared to be in good condition. A porch had been added to the front, and a freshly painted shed stood next to it. He scanned the garden, noting the types of vegetables she'd selected. Although too late in the summer to plant any, he could start reading up on them.

He knew nothing about gardening, nor had he cared to learn. For Jenna, he'd figure it out. He'd do the grunt work. She could reap the benefits. Unless, of course, she enjoyed getting her hands dirty. Then they could work together. Actually, he liked that idea better. It would give them a chance to talk.

A smile on his face, he pulled into her driveway and parked behind an older hatchback with a dent on the passenger side. Concern rushed over him. Had she been in an accident? He jumped from the car and hurried to her door. Before he got to the porch, Jenna stepped out with two large boxes stacked precariously in her arms.

"Jenna?"

She sucked in a rough breath, and the top box tumbled to the ground. The sound of smashing glass followed.

"My China!" She shoved the first box into his hands and opened the one that had fallen. Her shoulders slumped. "Broken. I knew I should've taken the time to wrap them in newspaper."

He placed the box he held on to the plastic chair next to the door. "It's my fault. I startled you. I'm sorry."

She gave the ruined dishes one last glance, then pushed to her feet. "Well, I shouldn't have been carrying so much, but I'm on a deadline. I need to be out of my house before sunset, and I can't fit very many boxes in my car." She motioned behind her. "Look at all the stuff I need to move yet, and it's already after three."

Stacks of boxes and dozens of garbage bags filled the room behind her. He looked from them to her. "You're moving?"

She tucked her hair behind her ear and nodded. "Unfortunately. Michael found out about my mated status and ordered me off our lands before nightfall." She sighed. "I've made three trips already, but I'm never going to get everything out in time, and nobody is allowed to help me since I'm no longer a Tanner."

His mom hadn't mentioned Jenna dropping stuff off at his old house, and he'd been at the new place all day. "Where did you take them?"

"Ummm, my apartment."

"Your apartment?" A brick landed in his gut. "Aren't you moving in with me?"

"No." She cocked her head to the side. "Why would I?"

"Because you're my mate. That's where you belong."

The icy indifference she'd worn for him the morning after they'd mated returned. "Are you evoking mating law?"

Which guaranteed him complete control over her, from deciding who she could associate with to whether or not they would have children. The antiquated law stemmed from a time when taking a mate was viewed as a necessity and a liability. The Kagan pack no longer followed the old dictates, but the Tanner pack did.

He shoved his hand into his pocket and toyed with the ring he'd driven five hours to get. Specially made by a coven of witches, the diamond band would mold to whichever form the wearer took, so it would never have to be removed. He had platinum wedding bands sitting in his dresser at home too. At the moment, it appeared as if he'd jumped the gun buying them.

"No." He let the ring settle against the key to their house. "I'm not going to force you to live with me. I just assumed you would."

"And I assumed you regretted me." She crossed her arms over her chest. "It's been a week, and this is the first I've heard from you."

"I figured I only had one chance to convince you to forgive me after the way I reacted. I didn't want to blow it."

She studied him for a long moment, then cleared her throat. "Why did you treat me so coldly?"

"I acted on my instincts and mated you without even knowing your name. I was afraid I'd only mated you because..." He exhaled slowly. "Because without Nic here, I felt the need to secure my position within the pack so I can take over."

"And by mating me, you feel as if you've betrayed your pack mate?"

"Yes. Being alpha is his destiny, not mine. Though, for the foreseeable future, I'll have to pretend it's my destiny."

Her gaze mapped his face as if she was trying to understand his statement by reading his expression. "Pretend?"

"Yeah." He rubbed at the back of his neck. Nobody was supposed to know he was faking his interest in leading, but Jenna was his mate. He refused to lie to her. "I'm only doing it to keep the peace between our dominants, so they don't start fighting among themselves without Nic here. As soon as he returns, I'm stepping aside."

She worried her lip between her teeth. He wanted to nibble on her tender flesh for her. She let her lip slip free before he gave in to the urge. "How long do you think he'll be gone?"

"Not sure. Years, probably." Riley had given no indication of leaving until she finished vet school. Once she had her degree, she might. Or not. Sean certainly wouldn't influence her. He cared about Riley's happiness too. Unfortunately, he couldn't give her what she wanted—a future with Nic.

"Years would be good. My cousin Ben matures soon. He can move away then. It'll be perfect." Jenna's eyes brightened.

"It will?"

"Yes." Jenna rushed forward and gave him a hug. "Thank you."

Her softness pressed against his body stirred his hunger, but curiosity over her reaction kept it at bay. "I'm glad you're okay with the idea of living a lie, but why thank me for it?"

"Because Michael threatened me. Told me I needed to convince you to take over your pack. He wants your pack as an ally, not a rival. With me as alpha female, he'd have that. Now I don't have to lie."

Sean tensed. "He threatened you? How? Tell me. Then I'll rip his throat out."

Jenna fisted his shirt and tipped her head back. "And if you do that, you'll end up as the alpha of my screwed-up pack. You don't want that. Isn't that what you said?"

He leaned closer and brushed his cheek against hers. Her scent filled his lungs. The anger choking him lessened. Peace settled over him. "No, I don't. Thank you for reminding me before I did something I'd regret. I'd make a horrible alpha no matter how I came about the role."

She rested her fingertips against his jaw. "If fate demanded it, you would make a wonderful alpha."

"You don't know me. How can you say that?"

She laid her other hand over her heart. "I carry a piece of your soul, Sean. I know."

A lump formed in his throat. He swallowed past it and blinked several times to ease the burn in his eyes. "You figured out my name?"

"Noah stopped by to congratulate me."

"I should've called. I was just busy getting our new house ready. I wanted everything perfect for you."

"You bought a house?"

"Well, I can't expect you to live with my parents, especially if we make a baby next month."

The color drained from her face. "I don't want kids. I should've told you."

Her words rushed out, and her breathing quickened. He cupped her face in his hands. "Okay. We won't have any then. My brothers can carry on our family line."

"You're okay with it?" A considering look passed over her face. "Mating law demands a female birth at least one son."

He shrugged. "Well, it's a stupid rule. I'm not going to force you to have my kid if you don't want one."

"Really?"

"Yes, really, but I'm curious. Why don't you want any kids?"

"I'd make a horrible mother. I'm too focused on my studies, and…" She lowered her gaze to his mouth. "I'm afraid my children will end up crazy like Michael. We carry the same genes."

He tipped up her chin. "Michael isn't crazy, nor was he always a bad alpha. I don't know why he stopped caring about his pack or why he became power hungry, but I can guarantee you're nothing like him and neither will any child that carries your genes be like him."

"You can't promise that. One night, Michael snapped. What if I —"

He pressed a finger to her lips. "Yes, I can. I trust my instincts, and I trust Noah. He said I couldn't have picked a better mate. I agree."

Tears collected on her lashes. "You're a good male, aren't you?"

"Would you have chosen a bad one to spend your life with?"

She grinned and shook her head. "No."

Sean dug out the ring, and the key to their house, then dropped to his knee. She stared at the diamond, and her eyes widened.

"I'm not asking you to marry me." Even though he wanted to drag her to the courthouse and make it official. She wasn't ready. Her reaction to him proved it. "I'm asking you to accept this promise ring and key. I want you to live with me and get to know me, then when you realize how amazing I am, you'll be my wife, not just my mate."

She fingered the three-carat ring and raised a brow. "This is a pretty expensive promise ring."

"You're worth it." He took it and poised it at the tip of her ring finger. "Say yes. Take a chance on love, Jenna."

"Yes"—she grinned—"but I'd rather take a chance on us."

He slid the ring into place and pulled her into his arms. "Then we win, because I won't ever give up on us."

The series continues with Nic

FOR A LIST OF AVAILABLE AND UPCOMING BOOKS, VISIT:

danaarcher.com

ABOUT THE AUTHOR

Dana Archer is Nancy Corrigan's discreet (closed-door) pen name.

Nancy is an author of paranormal romance and a storyteller of suspense and mystery. The result is a sexy, unforgettable love story. Her books have been recommended by top review sites such as The Library Journal, USA Today, RT Book Review, Night Owl Reviews and many more.

For more information, visit: DanaArcher.com

Nancy also writes under the pen name of Hayden Wolfe

Sean by Dana Archer

Discreet (closed door) version of Chance on Love by Nancy Corrigan

Published by:

Cherokee House Publishing LLC
325 N 10th St. Ste. 400, #247
Lewisburg, PA 17837